For Jan, even though he doesn't yet know
what a dedication is

Text and illustrations: Alexander Steffensmeier
© 2007 Patmos Verlag GmbH & Co. KG
Sauerländer Verlag, Düsseldorf
Translation copyright © 2007 by Patmos Verlag
First published as *Lieselotte im Schnee* in 2007 by Patmos Verlag, Germany

Published in the United States of America in 2008 by Walker Publishing Company, Inc.
Distributed to the trade by Macmillan

For information about permission to reproduce selections from this book, write to
Permissions, Walker & Company, 175 Fifth Avenue, New York, New York 10010

Library of Congress Cataloging-in-Publication Data available upon request
ISBN-13: 978-0-8027-9800-8 • ISBN-10: 0-8027-9800-4 (hardcover)
ISBN-13: 978-0-8027-9801-5 • ISBN-10: 0-8027-9801-2 (reinforced)

Visit Walker & Company's Web site at www.walkeryoungreaders.com

Printed in China
2 4 6 8 10 9 7 5 3 1 (hardcover)
2 4 6 8 10 9 7 5 3 1 (reinforced)

Millie in the Snow

Alexander Steffensmeier

Walker & Company
New York

As Christmas Day neared, Millie was very impatient at milking time each morning. There was so much else to do!

You see, Millie was not an ordinary cow. No, Millie was a . . .

...mail COW!

And since people always send one another so many letters and packages at Christmastime, Millie and the mail carrier had their hands and hooves full.

On Christmas Eve, it took
extra long to deliver the mail.

"Okay, that's everything," the mail carrier
said tiredly. "We can go home now."

Surprised, Millie looked at all the
packages that were still in her bag.

"Take them with you. They're for you and your friends at the farm," the mail carrier said.

"Get home safely. Maybe I'll pop by tonight for a glass of Christmas punch."

As the mail carrier zoomed home, he thought proudly about the presents he had left with Millie.

In the last few
weeks he had been
very busy.

He had made a big
cowbell for Millie . . .

There was a new
collar for the goat.

. . . and embroidered a coffeepot cover
and ordered a cool lava lamp for the farmer.

For the dog there was a comfortable
basket, and for the pigs
there were delicious
cookies.

... and even
found some
mistletoe—
just in case.

He had knitted a striped saddle
blanket for the little pony ...

After a quick pit stop in a nearby field, it was time for Millie to head home. But where was the path? The path was gone!

Completely gone.

Thank goodness she knew her way around so well. This meadow looked very familiar to her.

And that did too. Soon she would be home.

Oh no!

She must have been walking in circles.

She'd never get home that way.

From now on she would walk in a straight line.

In a *very* straight line.

Until . . .
uh-oh!

It was growing dark as Millie crossed
the stream light-hoovedly. If she didn't
find her way home soon, she would have
to spend Christmas Eve outside.

Now it was dark . . .

and creepy.

Time to move her tail—
and quickly!

All of a sudden, a giant monster appeared in front of Millie. Its mouth was wide open, and it wiggled its big red tongue.

"Moo-hoo!" cried Millie.

"What was that?" asked the farmer as she tied her shoelace. "Come on, let's get home!"

Millie struggled up a steep slope. How could she have wandered so far from home? Was she in the mountains already?

She took one last charge up the slope and . . .

"Home . . . I'm home!" thought Millie.

"Presents . . . PRESENTS!" thought all the others.

"Do the packages always have to arrive damaged?" sighed the farmer.

Everyone on the farm really liked the presents. Millie loved her practical udder warmer. And the farmer was so warm in her new poncho.

The mail carrier was a little surprised when he came for some Christmas punch. Still, as long as they all liked his gifts, he was happy.